The Sp
Tangle

Also by Alexander McCall Smith

Akimbo and the Elephants
Akimbo and the Lions
Film Boy
Uncle Gangster

Alexander McCall Smith

The Spaghetti Tangle

Illustrated by Elke Counsell

MAMMOTH

For Lucy

First published in Great Britain 1991
by Methuen Children's Books Ltd
Published 1992 by Mammoth
an imprint of Reed Consumer Books Limited
Michelin House, 81 Fulham Road, London SW3 6RB
and Auckland, Melbourne, Singapore and Toronto

Reprinted 1992, 1993, 1994

ISBN 0 7497 0937 5

A CIP catalogue record for this title
is available from the British Library

Printed and bound in Great Britain
by Cox & Wyman Ltd, Reading, Berkshire

Contents

1

Aunt Rebecca

There were once two children who had never eaten spaghetti. John and his sister Nicky, would have loved to have eaten spaghetti, but they were never allowed to do so much as taste it because of Aunt Rebecca.

John and Nicky had lived with their aunt for as long as they could remember. Their parents were experts on volcanoes, which is about one of the most dangerous jobs there is. They had to live in far-off places, waiting for volcanoes to erupt so that they could tell people what to do about it. It was far too dangerous a life for children and they had reluctantly had to pass John and Nicky over to Aunt Rebecca.

Aunt Rebecca was a kind-hearted person, in a funny sort of way, and the children were fond of her – also in a funny sort of way. They knew that, for some reason, she was not very happy with life but they had never been able to work out exactly why this was.

'I think she's grumpy because the person she wanted to marry her never did so,' said Nicky one day when Aunt Rebecca had been particularly grouchy. Their aunt had once told the children that she had been engaged to be married to somebody but that the wedding had been called off at the last moment. But she had not said more than that, and the whole thing remained a bit of a mystery.

Life with Aunt Rebecca was a little bit strange. It was not that she was always grumpy – she wasn't. But when she wasn't grumpy, she would almost certainly do rather odd things. For instance, they might find Aunt Rebecca in the sitting room, dancing to music. And it was not the sort of dancing that you might do by yourself, it was as if she was pretending to be dancing with somebody. She would have her arms held out before her, a dreamy look on her face, and she would whirl about the room just as if she were being guided by an invisible partner. This meant that the children were worried about bringing friends back to the house – just in case something embarrassing happened. And for this reason, they had fewer friends than other people. But they were fond enough of one another's company and they saw their friends at school.

Aunt Rebecca also had firm ideas about a

number of things, and the most important of these matters was food.

'People eat the most dreadful rubbish,' she would say. 'Look at all that terrible butter and sugar and other unhealthy things they put down their throats!'

Aunt Rebecca's idea of a healthy meal was carrot soup followed by raw cabbage and nuts and washed down with tomato juice. Now this was all very healthy, of course, and tasty too, but if you ate nothing else, then you began to want something different.

'Oh, for some chips!' John whispered to his sister as they sat down to their raw onion rings and diced turnip.

'I'd give anything for a piece of chocolate cake!' replied Nicky under her breath. 'With a twirl of cream on the top!'

'What was that!' barked Aunt Rebecca, looking sternly at the children. 'Did you say something about the onions?'

'No, Aunt,' said John in a sad voice. 'We said nothing about onions.'

'A fine vegetable the onion,' said Aunt Rebecca, peering at the pile of raw onion on her plate. 'It's very good for the blood, you know.'

'And they make you smell,' Nicky murmured.

'What?' snapped Aunt Rebecca. 'What was that?'

'I said, "And they keep you well",' said Nicky timidly.

10

'Indeed they do,' said Aunt Rebecca. 'Now eat up, children. There's a nice glass of carrot juice to follow.'

It was difficult for the children not to think about food. Every day, on their way home from school, they would pass the doors of the best restaurant in town. And every time they went past, their noses would catch the delicious cooking smells.

The children would have loved to eat in the restaurant, but how could they? Then, one Friday, Nicky had an extraordinary stroke of luck.

She had received a letter that morning from an uncle, who lived far away, but who always sent birthday presents. This year he had forgotten to do so and had written to tell her how sorry he was. And in the letter, to make up for the birthday present, he sent Nicky a crisp new banknote.

Nicky had never had so much money before and she found it difficult to make up her mind as to what to do with it.

'You could buy a new pen,' John suggested, as they walked home from school together.

'I've got a pen,' Nicky said.

'Or you could buy a game,' John went on.

'I don't want one,' said Nicky.

They were now just outside the restaurant. From within, there came the delicious smell of cooking, and they both stopped to sniff the air.

'I could take us to lunch,' Nicky said suddenly, her face breaking into a smile.

'Do you really want to?' John said, hardly daring believe the offer.

'Yes,' said Nicky, firmly. 'Let's go straight in.'

And they did.

2

A delicious discovery

'A table for two, please,' said Nicky to the waiter as he glided forward to meet them.

'Of course,' said the waiter politely. 'Would you please come with me.'

They followed him to a table near the window. There he drew out the chairs and invited them to sit down. Laid out on the table there was a crisp white tablecloth, shining silver knives and forks, and sparkling crystal glasses.

With a flourish the waiter produced the menu.

'I shall be back soon,' he said. 'I shall take your order then.'

Nicky opened the menu and looked at the list of dishes it contained. Many of them were written in French, and she had no idea what they were. Others were easier to understand. She knew what roast beef was and she had a good idea what chocolate meringue would look like. Then her

14

face fell. John noticed. 'What's wrong?' he asked.

'I've just seen what it all costs,' Nicky whispered. 'I haven't got nearly enough money.'

She passed the menu over to her brother. He turned pale as he read.

'There's nothing here that we can afford,' he said. 'We'll have to sneak out.'

They looked about them. Their table was far from the door and they would have to walk past everybody else if they were to leave.

'Come on,' said John, beginning to push his chair back. 'There's no point in staying.'

At that moment, the swing doors into the kitchen opened and out came the waiter. Smiling, he crossed the restaurant to stand at the side of their table.

'Well,' he said cheerfully. 'Have you had the time to make your choice?'

Nicky gazed down at the tablecloth.

'I'm sorry,' she said, in a small voice. 'We haven't got enough money. It all costs far too much.'

John braced himself for the waiter's anger.

The waiter said nothing for a few moments. Then, he leant forward, and whispered: 'How much have you got? You show me.'

Nicky took the note out of her pocket and showed it to him.

'Oh dear,' said the waiter. 'I can see that you have no idea how much restaurants cost.' He shook his head. 'Oh dear! Oh dear!'

'Don't worry,' said John. 'We'll go right now. And we're sorry for wasting your time.'

'Oh no you don't,' the waiter said. 'It's a rule at any really good restaurant that nobody goes out hungry. You were my guests the moment you stepped in the door, and I won't have my guests disappointed.'

'Do you really mean that?' asked Nicky.

'Of course I do,' said the waiter. 'Now, what I suggest is that we think of something that doesn't cost quite as much as the dishes on the menu. I'll get the chef to make it specially for you.'

The waiter thought for a moment, then he made his suggestion.

'I know!' he said. 'What about a good bowl of spaghetti. You could afford that.'

Nicky looked at John, who said nothing.

'Well,' said the waiter. 'You like spaghetti, don't you?'

'No,' said Nicky. 'I mean yes. I mean, well, we've never actually eaten spaghetti.'

The waiter straightened up in astonishment.

'You've never eaten spaghetti!' he exclaimed. 'Do you mean to say you've never even tasted it?'

'No,' said Nicky. 'We've never even tasted it. You see, we live with our Aunt, and she's the President of the Carrot and Nut League, and . . .'

The waiter cut her short.

'Let's waste no more time,' he said. 'Two spaghettis coming up!'

John and Nicky did not have to wait long. Within minutes, the waiter had placed before them two large plates of spaghetti, topped with generous helpings of thick sauce. The mere smell of the mouth-watering dish was almost enough for the children; but the taste, and the feel, and the longness of it . . . well, there are no words lengthy enough to describe all that.

At the end of the meal, with their plates scraped quite clean, Nicky paid and the two of

them said goodbye to the waiter.

'Come back one day,' the waiter said, with a smile.

Nicky nodded, but she knew that there was very little chance that they would be able to afford another meal. And as for John, he knew that it would be a long, long time, if ever, before they tasted spaghetti again.

3

A very special competition

It was back to carrot juice and raw onion again, with only the memory of that delicious spaghetti to keep them going. They tried to raise the subject of spaghetti with Aunt Rebecca, but it merely sent her into a rage.

'Certainly not!' she exploded. 'I'm not having that stuff in my kitchen. The mere thought of it!'

'But there's nothing wrong with spaghetti,' John pleaded. 'It's quite healthy.'

'But look what people put on it,' Aunt Rebecca replied heatedly. 'Thick red sauce, full of Heaven knows what! Oils, spices, grease, meat, and so on. No. Absolutely not.'

John gave up, and Nicky didn't even bother to argue with her aunt.

'One day,' she said to herself. 'One day I shall have spaghetti again. I know I shall!'

Several weeks later, John was reading a

magazine when something caught his eye. There on the page was a brightly coloured advertisement with a picture of a large bowl of spaghetti. The sight of the spaghetti made his mouth water as it brought back the memory of that marvellous meal in the restaurant. Then he read on, and he realised that here was their chance.

'Look,' he said to Nicky. 'We shall have to enter.'

Nicky took the advertisement and read it through. It had been inserted in the magazine by the manufacturers of Pipelli's Spaghetti, and this is what it said:

Spaghetti is best served with sauce, as we all know. But what sauce is best? Everybody has his or her favourite, so why not send us your recipe. We shall choose the one we think is best, and as a prize the winner will be invited to lunch with our chairman, Mr Pipelli, right here in our spaghetti works. You will see how spaghetti is made and you will even be able to try your hand at making some yourself! So enter straightaway!

Nicky glanced at John.

'Do you really think we could enter?' she said. 'Do you think we'd stand a chance?'

'Of course we would,' replied John. 'Somebody's got to win.'

'But what about a recipe?' asked Nicky. 'I don't

have a recipe for sauce.'

'I've already thought about that,' John said. 'Do you remember that sauce we had at the restaurant? Well, we could ask the chef if he would give us the recipe and if we could use it for the competition. It doesn't have to be your own invention – it only has to be your favourite recipe.'

Nicky was doubtful, but when John promised that he would do the asking at the restaurant, she agreed. Cutting the entry form out of the magazine, she tucked it into her pocket.

'What are you doing?' Aunt Rebecca asked sharply, but before Nicky could reply a pan of parsnips started to boil over in the kitchen and Aunt Rebecca had to dash off to deal with it.

'I can't wait,' John whispered. 'I've got a feeling that we're going to win.'

They went to the restaurant the next day. The waiter recognised them and gave them a warm smile of welcome.

'We're not here to have lunch,' said John. 'We're here for a recipe.'

The waiter was surprised, but when they explained what they had in mind he gave them a wink and told them to wait. A few minutes later, he came out of the kitchen with a piece of paper in his hand.

'The chef didn't mind at all,' he said. 'In fact, he was flattered by your request. Here's the recipe.'

Nicky took the recipe and studied it. Then they both thanked the waiter and left the restaurant.

'I hope you win,' he called out. 'And the chef hopes so too. He was very interested in the competition and he says that he will enter one of his other recipes as well. But don't worry – he's sure you've got the best one of all!'

4

Waiting to win

Nicky filled in the form and sent it off to the Pipelli Spaghetti Company. Then the waiting began. The advertisement had said that the results would be announced 'within three weeks', and to make sure that they didn't miss the announcement, the children pored over the newspaper every day. And every day they were disappointed.

'I don't know why you're suddenly so interested in the news,' Aunt Rebecca said. 'I'm sure you must be up to no good.'

Then, one Friday afternoon, John saw the item he had been waiting for. It was a small notice, tucked away in the corner of a page. 'The results of the Pipelli Spaghetti Competition will be published tomorrow,' it said. 'Make sure you don't miss them!'

John and Nicky could barely wait. When at last they saw the next day's newspaper, they opened

it with shaking hands. Sure enough, there on the front page was a large advertisement headed: Lucky Winner.

'I can't bear to read it,' Nicky said. 'I'll close my eyes. You read it and tell me if we've won.'

Nicky closed her eyes. There was a silence.

'Have we won?' she asked. 'Do tell me.'

She opened her eyes. John was staring glumly at the page.

'No,' he said. 'Somebody else won.'

He paused. Then, turning sadly to Nicky, he read out what was written in the paper:

There were hundreds and hundreds of entries in the spaghetti competition. Most of the recipes were very good indeed, although some were not. (Some were very bad.) At last the winner has been chosen and a letter has been sent to the fortunate person.'

Nicky looked thoughtful. 'But it could have been us,' she said. 'It doesn't say we didn't win. The letter could be on its way to *us*.'

John pondered what his sister said. She could be right. Perhaps there *was* a letter in the post for them. Perhaps it would arrive tomorrow, or the day after that.

So the next day they waited for the post to drop through the door. Rushing to pick it up, they quickly shuffled through the letters to see if there was anything for them. No. There were one or two bills, a magazine, and several letters from members of the Carrot and Nut League – nothing for them.

It was the same the following day, and the day after that.

'How long do letters take to arrive?' Nicky asked.

'I'm not sure,' replied John. 'Two or three days. Maybe more.'

He knew, though, that there was now no chance of their having won, and when nothing arrived through the post the next day he told

Nicky that there was no point in believing any longer that they might have won.

It was bitterly disappointing. They had known that there would have been hundreds of people entering in the competition, and they had known in their heart of hearts that it was very difficult to win a competition like that, and yet it seemed to them as if they might have come so very close.

'Never mind,' said John, trying to sound more cheerful. 'Whoever did win will be very pleased with the news.'

And after that, they did not talk about the competition any more. They also tried to forget about spaghetti, and to give up all thought of eating it again and they tried to avoid the restaurant. They now crossed the street before they reached it, so that they would not be forced to breathe in the delicious smells or see the diners at their tables. Then, a few days later, as they were walking past on the other side of the street, they heard a shout.

'Hello there!' cried a voice. 'Hello, you two!'

John spun round. There, standing in the door of the restaurant and beckoning them across the street, was their friend the waiter.

'I want to speak to you,' he shouted out.

Reluctantly, John and Nicky crossed the street to stand before the waiter.

'Where have you been?' he asked. 'I've been on the look-out for you.'

'We've been going home a different way,' explained John, without going on to tell him why this was.

'I see,' said the waiter. 'Anyway, the important thing is that I've found you.'

The waiter drew them into the doorway.

'I've got amazing news for you,' he confided. 'The chef won the spaghetti competition. Isn't that wonderful?'

John glanced at Nicky. So the chef was the lucky person after all. If only he had given them his recipe and kept theirs!

'And you're pleased?' asked the waiter.

'Of course,' said John bravely. 'Please tell him we've very happy for him.'

The waiter laughed. 'Happy for yourself, more likely. He can't go.'

John and Nicky looked puzzled.

'He can't visit the spaghetti factory,' said the waiter. 'He's far too busy. And so he wants you two to have his prize for him. He's been in touch with Mr Pipelli, who says that that's perfectly all right with him. All that you have to do is to arrange a time.'

John clapped his hands together with delight. He could scarcely believe their good luck. They had resigned themselves to losing the competition, and now it was just as if they had won. He was already beginning to imagine what the factory would be like and what he would say to

Mr Pipelli. And Nicky, although still astonished by their sudden stroke of good fortune, was thinking exactly the same thing.

5

A welcome from Mr Pipelli

Aunt Rebecca was not at all pleased.

'A spaghetti factory!' she exploded. 'Did you say a SPAGHETTI factory?'

'Yes,' said John. 'Mr Pipelli's Spaghetti Factory.'

'You can't go,' she said. 'I won't hear of it.'

'But why not?' Nicky pleaded. 'There's nothing wrong with spaghetti.'

'We've already discussed that,' said Aunt Rebecca. 'And you know my views. No. And that's all there is to it.'

John thought quickly.

'It is rude to turn down an invitation, isn't it?' he asked. He knew very well Aunt Rebecca was most particular about manners.

'Of course it is,' snapped his aunt. 'It's very rude, unless you've got a good reason.'

'Well,' said John. 'Mr Pipelli has invited us to have lunch with him in his factory. Surely it

31

would be rude to say no.'

Aunt Rebecca was cornered. Eventually, after a lot more grumbling, she had to accept that it would be impolite for John and Nicky not to go, and permission was given.

'Well done!' Nicky whispered to her brother. 'I can almost smell the spaghetti already!'

'What was that?' asked Aunt Rebecca suspiciously. 'What did you say?'

But, from the kitchen, there came a squeak from the pressure cooker, and Aunt Rebecca had to dash off to attend to a pot of fresh seaweed, which was now done just to a turn.

On the day of the visit, John and Nicky were ready well before the spaghetti factory car arrived. The driver settled them in their seats, and they began the long journey to the factory.

'You'll like Mr Pipelli,' the driver said. 'Everybody likes him the moment they meet him. You just wait and see.'

They drove for an hour or so before they arrived. It was a very large factory – much bigger than either of them had imagined – and over the front gate there was a great sign made out of metal letters: Pipelli's Spaghetti – The King of Spaghettis.

The car swept into the driveway and came to a halt outside the main office. Ushered into the entrance hall by the driver, the two visitors were shown to a door which said, quite simply, THE BOSS.

'Go on,' said the driver. 'Knock.'

And Nicky did.

The door flew open the moment Nicky's knuckle hit the wood. There, before them, stood a stout man in a checked suit. He had curly black hair, sparkling eyes, and a smile that seemed to split his face in two.

'Well, well,' he said. 'My two guests! Please come in!'

John and Nicky entered the room cautiously. It was a more splendid office than they had ever imagined. On the walls were large paintings of

Italy, framed in heavy gold frames. On the mantlepiece, above the marble fireplace, there were cups and trophies, and at the far end was a great wooden desk, on which stood a large gold pen-stand.

'Yes,' said Mr Pipelli, as if reading their

thoughts. 'It is a splendid room, and I have indeed made a great deal of money out of spaghetti.'

'I didn't mean to stare,' John said apologetically. 'It's just that I've never seen . . .'

'But you are here to stare,' Mr Pipelli protested. 'That's why I invited you. Today you may stare and stare as much as you like, and nobody will think it the slightest bit odd!'

The driver had been right. Both John and Nicky liked Mr Pipelli immediately. Whenever he spoke he smiled, and when he wasn't speaking, his eyes twinkled with merriment. He was just the sort of person who would run a competition like this, and he was just the sort of person who would make sure that the winners had fun.

'Well,' said Mr Pipelli, rubbing his hands together. 'Let's go and take a look at the works. I've been in the spaghetti business for twenty years, you know, and I feel as excited by what goes on here as I was the day I started. So let's not wait any longer! Let's go and take a look at how spaghetti is made!'

They walked out of Mr Pipelli's office and made their way along a passageway that led into the heart of the factory. At the end of the passageway there was a door, which Mr Pipelli opened with a flourish.

'In this very room,' he said, his voice lowered in awe, 'we see the very beginnings of spaghetti.'

John and Nicky craned their necks to see

beyond Mr Pipelli. They were standing in the entrance to a large room in the centre of which stood a gigantic mound of flour. From this mound, people in white overalls were taking heaped shovels to pour into great metal mixers. As the flour was shovelled in, white clouds rose like steam, making the faces of the workers seem as pale as if they had just seen ghosts.

'A dusty business at this stage,' remarked Mr Pipelli, taking out a large silk handkerchief with which to remove the fine layer of flour that had already settled on the front of his suit.

John and Nicky followed the spaghetti

Olive Oil for Go !

manufacturer as he led them across to the mixing machines. At the side of each bowl there was a woman with a watering can. As each spadeful of flour was put into the bowl, she tipped her can over the edge and poured in a stream of thick, greenish liquid.

'Olive oil,' explained Mr Pipelli. 'It's very important in the making of spaghetti. And these ladies know exactly how much olive oil to put in each bowl. They all come from the same part of Italy – every one of them – where everybody, absolutely everybody, knows all there is to know about olive oil!'

John looked at the woman beside the bowl, who smiled at him, winked, and before he knew what was happening had tossed back her head, opened her mouth, and poured a stream of olive oil right down her throat!

John looked aghast, but Mr Pipelli just laughed.

'Don't worry about that,' he said. 'They live on olive oil. There's nothing they like better.'

He nodded to the woman as they began to move on.

'Thank you, Olive,' he said. 'And do take the rest of the day off, if you wish!'

As they went on, Mr Pipelli turned to the children and whispered.

'She won't take the day off,' he explained. 'She loves her job so much that she'll want to stay. This is a very happy factory, you see!'

6

Things go wrong

'Next,' said Mr Pipelli as they prepared to leave the room. 'Next we shall see what happens to the dough. This is the really exciting part!'

Wondering what they were going to see next, John and Nicky followed their host through a door into another large room. This room was much noisier, as it was filled by a large machine, which was shuddering and shaking and making the most peculiar squelchy sound.

'This,' said Mr Pipelli proudly, 'is the actual spaghetti-making machine! This is the very heart of the factory.'

John and Nicky gazed at the giant machine. At one end, there was an open bowl, almost the size of a swimming pool, into which the dough which had been mixed next door was being loaded in great sticky globules. From that, a number of thick pipes led into the machine itself, one side of which was covered with a variety of dials and levers. Then, at the far end of the machine, more people in white uniforms were bustling about, taking strands of finished spaghetti in their hands like bundles of wool.

'This is the spaghetti spinner,' explained Mr Pipelli, proudly. 'It is, in fact, the most advanced and expensive spaghetti spinner in the world. Not only can it make spaghetti, it can make macaroni, canelloni, tagliatelli and every other shape of pasta you could dream of!'

Mr Pipelli's expression had become dreamy.

'Just the names of all the pastas make my mouth water,' he said. 'Just think of them! *Capellini! Quadretinni! Nastrini! Farfallette!*'

He closed his eyes in ecstasy before he remembered that he had visitors and came back to earth. With a look of pride, he pointed to the other side of the room.

'And that's the finished product being hung up to dry,' he said. 'That's only a week's output of spaghetti – enough to supply an entire city for at least a year!'

John and Nicky gazed at the towering white racks on which the spaghetti had been hung up to dry. You could get lost in that, John thought; and if you did, it would be like being in a spaghetti forest.

Mr Pipelli made his way towards the machine, beckoning the children to follow him.

'These dials control the shape,' he said, pointing to a line of the buttons and wheels along the side of the machine.

He turned and whispered in Nicky's ear.

'Have you ever seen twisty spaghetti?' he asked.

Nicky shook her head.

'Then watch,' said Mr Pipelli, fiddling with one of the dials.

As the dials turned, the noise inside the machine seemed to change briefly and within a few seconds the most amazing twisty spaghetti began to emerge at the other end.

Mr Pipelli turned to John, beaming with pride.

'I'm the only person in the world who makes that,' he said. 'Now, what about you? Would you like to try a special shape?'

John reached forward to the dial and began to turn it gingerly.

'A little bit more to the left,' prompted Mr Pipelli. 'Now to the right.'

Nicky watched with fascination as the machine began to respond to her brother's instructions.

'It's round!' she cried out. 'Round spaghetti!'

Mr Pipelli cast a glance at the place where the spaghetti was emerging.

'Well!' he exclaimed. 'What an interesting shape. Perhaps we'll have to make more of that.'

John craned his neck to see the results of his adjustment. The round spaghetti was certainly very interesting, and tasty-looking too, but

perhaps it was a little bit too short.

'Can I make it longer?' he asked.

'Anything you wish,' said Mr Pipelli. 'Just pull that lever over there.'

John gave the lever a tug.

'Not so far!' shouted Mr Pipelli, but it was too late. The machine gave a shudder and started to whine. Almost immediately, from the other end, immensely long strands of spaghetti began to shoot out. In fact, they were so long that they appeared to have no end at all.

'Cable spaghetti!' moaned Mr Pipelli, rushing around and throwing his hands in the air. 'Exactly what every spaghetti manufacturer dreads more than anything else!'

It took Mr Pipelli a minute or two to recover himself. During this time, the machine continued to spew out the strands of endless spaghetti. At the other end, the spaghetti workers frantically tried to pick up the growing mounds of spaghetti strands, but no sooner did they manage to shift some of them than the machine produced more than they had taken away. It was a hopeless task.

Then, when at last he began to calm down, Mr Pipelli managed to find the switch which turned the machine off. With a last heave and gurgle, the giant spaghetti-making device squeezed out the last few feet of spaghetti and became silent.

Mr Pipelli mopped his brow.

'Don't worry,' he said to John. 'That wasn't your

fault. This machine's been faulty for a good few months. It was bound to do that sooner or later.'

John was relieved to hear this. He had been certain it was all his fault.

'We'll have to try and deal with all that spaghetti,' said Mr Pipelli. 'Then I intend to do something about fixing this machine.'

Mr Pipelli now took John and Nicky to stand beside the vast mountain of spaghetti.

'It's going to be rather difficult,' he said despondently. 'We'll have to find the ends of the strands – then we'll have to roll this all up. That's the only way to do it.'

John and Nicky looked at the spaghetti. It seemed like an impossible task to sort out the muddle of strands, and yet, as John looked, he saw what looked like an end. Cautiously he reached down and picked it up.

'Well done!' said Mr Pipelli. 'Now just pull on it.'

John did as he was told and gradually drew out a long strand of spaghetti. It seemed to go on forever and soon he was standing at the other end of the room, linked to the pile of spaghetti by a long, slithery strand.

While this was happening, Nicky had spotted another end which she took hold of and began to draw out. Soon she was standing by John's side while Mr Pipelli went off to a storeroom to look for something to wind it round. After a few minutes he came back, carrying an empty barrel. Then, closely supervised by Mr Pipelli, the children began the slippery task of winding the still-wet spaghetti on to the barrel. It was slow work, as the spaghetti kept getting twisted and knotted up, but at last it was finished and the mountain of spaghetti began to look much smaller.

'We shall let the spaghetti workers do all the rest,' said Mr Pipelli, who was beginning to look very much more cheerful. 'Now, let's take a look at this machine. Does either of you know anything about machinery?'

John and Nicky shook their heads. They could put the chain back on a bicycle – but you would have to know a great deal more than that to be able to fix something as complicated as a spaghetti-making machine.

Mr Pipelli looked slightly disappointed.

'Oh dear,' he said. 'I don't know much about it myself. Still, we can have a go!'

7

Tangled up

John and Nicky watched quietly as Mr Pipelli picked up a screwdriver and began to unscrew a metal plate on the side of the machine.

'This is the inspection hatch,' he explained cheerfully. 'It allows us to get inside the works.'

John looked doubtfully at Nicky and gulped. What would be inside that great, gleaming machine? And what could they possibly do inside it? Was Mr Pipelli quite sure that it was turned off completely?

Mr Pipelli unscrewed the last screw and put the screwdriver down. Then, carefully taking hold of the edges of the plate, he took it off and laid it down on the floor.

John and Nicky peered through the hatch.

'It's very dark inside,' ventured John. 'Perhaps we should call a mechanic. He might know where everything is.'

Mr Pipelli chuckled. 'Why go to all that trouble and expense?' he said breezily. 'Most machines are quite simple once you work out what's what. And as for the darkness, there's a torch here. So let's go in.'

Mr Pipelli led the way, and he was followed by Nicky. John brought up the rear.

'I'm scared,' whispered Nicky. 'What if somebody turned the machine on while we were in here?'

John did not try to answer her question. Yet there was no doubt in his mind that they would be in very serious trouble if that happened. All about them there were rollers, sifters, crushers, and squeezers. The squeezers looked particularly dangerous, and John thought that anybody who got caught up in one of those would stand a very good chance of looking rather like a piece of spaghetti when they eventually got him out.

'You've no need to worry about that,' said Mr Pipelli jovially. 'It's impossible to turn the machine on when the inspection hatch is open. Now, we've got to locate the bit that controls the length. Can anybody see it?'

John looked up and at that precise moment a large blob of unsqueezed spaghetti dough fell down the back of his neck.

'Perhaps we should be wearing overalls,' said Mr Pipelli, noticing what had happened. 'Still, one can't expect to visit a spaghetti factory and not get a little bit of spaghetti here and there!'

Mr Pipelli flashed his torch about him. Suddenly he let out a cry of triumph.

'That's it,' he said. 'That's where the problem is.'

The children looked at the place where the beam of light was resting. High up at the top of the machine, the spaghetti had become hopelessly tangled. It was like a giant ball of knitting that had gone terribly wrong.

Mr Pipelli passed the torch to John to hold while he tried to pull down the tangle, but try as he might he could not quite reach high enough. After he had failed three times he stood back and scratched his head.

'I know what we'll do,' he said, after a while. 'You climb on my shoulders, John, and we'll do it that way.'

Nicky held the torch while John clambered on to Mr Pipelli's shoulders. Then, as Mr Pipelli moved into position, John began to tug at the mess of spaghetti.

It was not easy work. The spaghetti was sticky and had wound itself round and round in a maze of loops and knots. John tugged and pulled, only pausing to wipe strands of spaghetti off his face. And all the time, he heard Mr Pipelli huffing and puffing beneath him, trying to keep him in the right position. Then, just as he had pulled off the last strand, Mr Pipelli's legs gave out from underneath him and John found himself tumbling

down, closely followed by the great ball of spaghetti he had just dislodged.

The spaghetti was soft, of course, which was a good thing, but when John got up he was covered in it from head to toe.

'I'm terribly sorry,' said Mr Pipelli, nonetheless still sounding very cheerful. 'But at least we've fixed the machine. I'm sure it'll work now!'

'But what about me?' John mumbled from somewhere within the tangle of spaghetti. 'I'm afraid I'm all tied up.'

Mr Pipelli flashed the torch over John.

'I see,' he said. 'Yes, well maybe we should do something about you. Now, I'll just start pulling on this piece here . . .'

Mr Pipelli took hold of a strand of spaghetti and began to tug. As he did so, John felt the spaghetti slithering around him, like the coils of an impossibly long snake.

'That's it!' said Mr Pipelli enthusiastically. 'It's coming away nicely.'

Mr Pipelli spoke too soon. Although the spaghetti had begun to move, it had also begun to tighten.

'Please stop,' John called out. 'It's tying me up so that I can't move.'

Mr Pipelli shook his head.

'We'll have to get you out of here somehow,' he said. 'Then we can have a better look at the problem.'

Helped by Nicky, Mr Pipelli managed to half roll, half push John out of the hatch and back into the factory. The spaghetti workers stood round, gazing at John, scratching their heads.

'Can anybody think of a way to get him out of there?' asked Mr Pipelli. 'If we pull at the spaghetti it seems just to get worse.'

The spaghetti workers whispered among themselves. They had seen all sorts of things happen in the spaghetti factory. They remembered the day when Mr Pipelli dropped his hat into the spaghetti machine and had watched helplessly as it had come out the other end in long strands of material. They all remembered that very well and still talked about it whenever they saw their employer wearing anything on his head. In fact, one of the spaghetti workers had called her new baby Cappello, which means 'hat' in Italian – just to remind her of that marvellous incident. Yes, they had seen many strange things, but never anything quite as strange as this.

As they were standing about, wondering how they could possibly get John out of the tangle, one of the women suddenly stepped forward and whispered something in Mr Pipelli's ear. It was Olive.

Mr Pipelli listened gravely, stroked his chin, and then nodded.

'That might just work, Olive,' he said. 'You just go and fetch the – you know what I mean – and we'll try.'

Nicky tugged at Mr Pipelli's sleeve.

'What are you going to do?' she asked timidly. 'You're not going to hurt him are you? Aunt Rebecca will be furious if you do.'

Mr Pipelli patted her gently on the shoulder.

'Of course not,' he said reassuringly. Then, whispering, he went on to explain. 'Olive suggested that we –' his eyes glistened with mischief '– that we pour olive oil all over him. In that way he'll be slippery enough to wriggle his way out of the spaghetti! Now, isn't that a brilliant idea?'

Before Nicky had the chance to reply, Olive had returned. Fortunately, John could not see out of the spaghetti tangle and so he was unable to watch them raise the large can over his head and begin to pour. The first thing he knew of it was when he felt the cold, slippery oil slithering its way all over him.

'Now!' shouted Mr Pipelli. 'Wriggle!'

John did as he was told and, after a few moments of wriggling and hopping, he felt himself begin to slip out of the tangle. With a final shiver and shake, he popped out of the tangle and was free. As he did so, all the spaghetti workers raised a cheer of delight.

John was thrilled to be free of the spaghetti. In fact, he was so pleased, that he hardly noticed the fact that he was covered, not only with little bits

of spaghetti, but with olive oil too.

Mr Pipelli beamed with pleasure.

'Now, we can try the machine again,' he said. 'Let's see if we've fixed it.'

It took only one press on the button. With a great whirring the machine came back to life, working perfectly.

'We did it!' shouted Mr Pipelli. 'Everybody take a day's holiday!'

The spaghetti workers gave another rousing cheer and Mr Pipelli turned to John and Nicky.

'And as for you, my friends,' he said. 'Let's go straight to the factory kitchen and have lunch. I've asked the chef to cook the very best plate of spaghetti he can manage, so I can assure you it should be most delicious.'

Mr Pipelli was right. The lunch was even tastier than the one which John and Nicky had eaten in the restaurant. There was not just one plate of spaghetti for each person – there were six! There was:

For the first course:

Spaghetti with special cheese sauce, made out of Swiss cheese with holes. The spaghetti was threaded through the holes of the cheese and tied in bows!

For the second course:

A single strand of spaghetti ten yards long. This strand was curled round and round on the plate and had to be sucked up into the mouth and swallowed all in one piece!

For the third course:

Spaghetti which was plain on the outside but which had the sauce inside the hollow centre. Many tried to make such spaghetti, but only Mr Pipelli could do it.

For the fourth course:

Indian cobra spaghetti. This spaghetti stood up on end like a cobra. It swayed as you tried to eat it, but was very delicious when caught.

For the fifth course:

Needle spaghetti. This spaghetti was so thin that you could suck it into your mouth through the spaces in between your teeth!

For the sixth, and final course:

Ordinary spaghetti in the most delicious red sauce imaginable. There was oodles of sauce, which had to be slurped up with the spaghetti. Everybody made a great noise doing this, and got covered with sauce, more or less from head to toe. Second helpings were served – twice!

Afterwards, as full and as happy as they had ever been in their lives, the children were led by Mr Pipelli to the front door and ushered into a waiting car.

'Thank you so much for all your help,' he said, as he shook hands with them. 'And perhaps we shall meet again one day. After all, who knows what life can bring?'

The car drew away from the factory, with Mr Pipelli still standing on the steps, waving his handkerchief at his departing guests. Inside the car, John and Nicky were happier than they had been for years. It didn't matter that John had a blob of spaghetti dough lodged down the back of his shirt. It did not matter that the rest of his clothes were covered with sticky strands of spaghetti as well as being soaked in olive oil. Nor did it matter that Nicky's dress was splattered with hundreds of reminders of the red sauce. It had been a marvellous, exciting day and they both knew they would remember every moment of it forever.

8

Aunt Rebecca gets to work

'Look at you!' hissed Aunt Rebecca, quivering with rage. 'Just look at you!'

John hung his head. He had to admit that he looked a bit of a sight, covered as he was with spaghetti, but surely it would all wash off easily enough?

'And as for you, Nicky,' Aunt Rebecca went on. 'What were you doing letting your brother get himself into such a state? And look at your dress – ruined!'

'I was holding a torch!' Nicky said timidly. 'Mr Pipelli had John on his shoulders, you see . . .'

'On his what?' cried Aunt Rebecca. 'You both obviously have a great deal of explaining to do!'

John tried to tell his aunt about what happened, but it only seemed to make matters worse. At the end of his explanation, her face was stormy with anger.

'I should have known that something like this would happen,' she said. 'Nothing good could be expected of a spaghetti factory! And as for that Mr Pipelli, I very much hope that he has a good explanation when I see him tomorrow.'

'You're seeing him tomorrow?' Nicky asked. 'But why?'

'To complain,' snapped Aunt Rebecca. 'Do you think I'm going to let him get away with all this?'

John and Nicky remained silent. When Aunt Rebecca was in that sort of mood, they knew there was nothing they could do to persuade her otherwise.

The next day Aunt Rebecca told John and Nicky to get ready to accompany her to Mr Pipelli's factory. They were very unwilling to go, as the last thing they wanted to do was to complain to the generous and likeable Mr Pipelli, but their aunt insisted.

They arrived at the factory in sunken spirits.

'It's going to be awful,' Nicky whispered to John. 'She's going to make a terrible scene.'

'I know,' said John under his breath. 'And Mr Pipelli will think that we put her up to it.'

The man at the factory gate tried to tell Aunt Rebecca that it would be impossible for her to see Mr Pipelli, but she brushed him aside.

'If you don't show me to his office,' she said, 'then I shall find my own way there.'

The man looked Aunt Rebecca up and down and decided that she was not a person to be trifled with. Reluctantly he led the three of them to the door marked THE BOSS.

Aunt Rebecca knocked once, but did not wait for an answer. Throwing the door wide open, she burst into Mr Pipelli's room and marched up to the astonished spaghetti manufacturer's desk.

Mr Pipelli sprang to his feet and, hiding his surprise, bowed to Aunt Rebecca.

'My dear lady,' he said, reaching for her hand. 'How kind of you to call on me. I take it that you're the aunt of my two friends.'

Aunt Rebecca stopped in her tracks.

'Please,' said Mr Pipelli, kissing her hand. 'Please allow me to offer you a chair.'

By now, Aunt Rebecca, overcome by the politeness and charm of the famous spaghetti manufacturer, was completely incapable of complaining.

'Actually,' she began. 'I was rather ... er ... rather cross ... '

She stopped. Mr Pipelli had now seated her in a chair and had offered her a peppermint from a silver bowl on his desk.

'I don't eat sweets,' said Aunt Rebecca.

'But how wise!' said Mr Pipelli. 'If only other people would do the same as you.'

Aunt Rebecca looked suspiciously at Mr Pipelli.

'But I don't see how you can say that,' she said.

'After all, you make all that spaghetti which people cover with red sauce and terrible things like that.'

Mr Pipelli waved a hand in the air.

'Well perhaps you could help me,' he said, smiling in a charming way. 'I've always wanted to make a healthier sort of spaghetti, but I've never found quite the right recipe.'

For the first time that day, Aunt Rebecca smiled.

'Perhaps I could help,' she said, warming to his idea. 'Perhaps I could invent . . . carrot-flavoured spaghetti!'

Mr Pipelli clapped his hands together.

'My dear lady,' he said. 'What a brilliant idea! Please, please, do that for me. I should be most grateful if you did.' And at that, Mr Pipelli rose to his feet and kissed her hand again, making Aunt Rebecca look down at the floor and blush.

Aunt Rebecca was quite silent on the way back home. When they reached the house, the two children watched her as she made straight for the kitchen and closed the door behind her.

'She really means it,' said Nicky. 'She really intends to invent carrot-flavoured spaghetti.'

'It'll taste awful,' said John. 'The only people who will even think about eating it will be the members of the Carrot and Nut League.'

Aunt Rebecca remained in the kitchen for the

rest of the day. She came out briefly at lunch time, to hand the two children a plate of lettuce sandwiches to eat, but she seemed too preoccupied to talk.

At four o'clock in the afternoon, John began to worry. He knocked at the door and asked her if she was all right, but he received no more than a grunt in reply. At five o'clock he knocked again, and this time Aunt Rebecca opened the door and peered out at him.

'Yes,' she said. 'What is it?'

'I was wondering if you were all right,' John said. 'We haven't seen you all day.'

Aunt Rebecca dried her hands on her apron.

'I'm perfectly all right,' she said. 'And dinner will be at the normal time — seven on the dot.' Then she closed the door.

9

Mr Pipelli pops the question

John and Nicky were sitting at the table at five minutes before seven. At seven o'clock exactly, the door from the kitchen opened and Aunt Rebecca came out carrying a large bowl from which a small cloud of steam was rising. It was obvious to the children that this was not a dish of raw onions or lettuce salad. But what could it be?

'Spaghetti,' announced Aunt Rebecca simply. 'You tell me how much you like the stuff, and so I've made you some.'

Nicky's mouth fell open with surprise.

'Spaghetti?' she exclaimed. 'Real spaghetti?'

'Yes,' said Aunt Rebecca proudly. 'What is more, this is the first bowl, the very first bowl, of carrot-flavoured spaghetti. I've just invented it, and I shall introduce that Pipelli man to it tomorrow.'

John and Nicky watched suspiciously as the

newly-invented spaghetti was ladled on to their plates. It looked like ordinary spaghetti in shape, but it was undeniably carrot-coloured.

'Eat up,' said Aunt Rebecca. 'It won't taste nearly so good if you let it get cold.'

Reluctantly John and Nicky wound the yellow strands around their forks and then passed it to their mouths. Then they looked down at their plates, and after that at one another.

'Well?' asked Aunt Rebecca. 'What do you think?'

'It's marvellous,' said John.

'Wonderful!' said Nicky.

And they meant it. Aunt Rebecca had invented the most delicious spaghetti they had ever tasted. It was a miracle, and they had been right there in the house when it had happened. Without a break they finished off the rest of the spaghetti before them and then passed the empty plates to their aunt for more.

'My word!' exclaimed Aunt Rebecca, her face breaking out into a contented smile. 'That's the first time you've asked for more – ever!'

Aunt Rebecca telephoned Mr Pipelli the next morning and invited him to the house for lunch. He agreed to come, and when he arrived at the front door he had presents for everyone. John and Nicky each received a fountain pen with a real gold nib, and for Aunt Rebecca there was a

bouquet of red roses. She became quite speechless when he gave these to her, and when he bent and kissed her hand again the children noticed that she blushed so much that she made the roses look pale.

The new spaghetti was served for lunch. Everyone eagerly awaited Mr Pipelli's reaction, and when it came they were not disappointed. As he took the first mouthful his eyes rolled up to the ceiling in ecstasy. Then, on the second mouthful, he threw his hands up, leapt to his feet, and tossed his table napkin out of the window in his excitement.

'It is magnificent!' he said, when he had recovered enough to speak. 'We shall start manufacturing this spaghetti immediately.'

He sat down and looked seriously at Aunt Rebecca.

'You have done the world of spaghetti making a great service,' he said solemnly. 'And that will never be forgotten. Never!'

'What a nice man you are,' said Aunt Rebecca, 'for a spaghetti manufacturer,' she added. 'Would you care to join us for lunch tomorrow?'

Mr Pipelli nodded his head enthusiastically and said that this would give him the greatest pleasure. John felt that he should warn him that lunch could well be raw onions and seaweed, but he did not have the opportunity to speak to him privately.

John need not have worried. Mr Pipelli sat at the table the following day and ate his raw onions with every appearance of pleasure. At the end, to the astonishment of the two children, he asked for more.

'Quite delicious,' Mr Pipelli said, smacking his lips rather loudly. 'And so positively good for the system.'

'Absolutely,' said Aunt Rebecca, as she ladled more onions on to her visitor's plate.

Mr Pipelli came back to lunch the next day, and the day after that. He and Aunt Rebecca seemed to get on very well, and they always took a walk round the garden after the meal. There Mr Pipelli would pick roses from Aunt Rebecca's rosebushes (something she normally never allowed anybody to do) and would present them to her with a low bow.

Finally, exactly one week later, Mr Pipelli announced that he had invited Aunt Rebecca to marry him and that she had agreed. They would be married the following Saturday and would all move into his mansion near the spaghetti factory.

'Your charming aunt will become Mrs Pipelli,' he said proudly. 'And you, my dear children, will become my step-nephew and step-niece. You can stay with us until your parents have found all the volcanoes they can. After all, there can't be that many. That is, of course, if you agree to this little change in your lives.'

'Of course we do,' shouted Nicky, and kissed Aunt Rebecca on the cheek. Aunt Rebecca smiled. She seemed much less severe now – it was almost as if she had caught Mr Pipelli's habit of beaming with pleasure at everything he saw.

Because she was in such a good mood, later that day John decided to ask Aunt Rebecca about the last time she had been engaged to be married.

'It was all a very long time ago,' she explained. 'He was a pastry chef, you know – a very good one. He was a kind man too.'

'Then what happened?' asked John. 'Did he run away?'

For a moment or two Aunt Rebecca looked sorrowful again, as if she were remembering something rather sad.

'No,' she said. 'He didn't run away. It's just that he was rather ... greedy. In fact, he was terribly, terribly greedy. When we ate meals together, he would take things from my plate and pop them into his mouth. I don't think he even knew he was doing it.'

She paused, dabbing at a tear which had appeared in the corner of her eye.

'He made our wedding cake himself,' she said. 'It was the most beautiful cake you can imagine. It was covered with at least four bowls of marzipan and there were six tiers of white icing. Then, the day before the wedding, when I knew that the cake would be finished, I went round to look at it.

And that's when I changed my mind.'

John wondered what Aunt Rebecca could possibly have seen to make her call off the wedding.

'There he was,' she said. 'He was sitting in his kitchen, looking very pleased with himself. And do you know what he had done? *He had eaten the cake – every last crumb of it*!'

'All six tiers?' asked Nicky, astonished that one person could be so greedy as to eat his own wedding cake – before the wedding.

'Yes,' said Aunt Rebecca grimly. 'And when he saw me, he looked very guilty. So I said to him: Octavius Hunt (for that was what he was called), you will have to find somebody else to marry you I'm afraid! You are far, far too greedy for me!'

'Mr Pipelli would never do anything like that,' said John.

At the mention of Mr Pipelli's name, Aunt Rebecca cheered up.

'Of course he wouldn't,' she said, closing her eyes dreamily. 'What a marvellous man he is!'

From that day on, Aunt Rebecca was a different person. She never scowled, she was cheerful all day, and everything about her seemed so much brighter. But, most remarkable of all, was the change which occurred in Aunt Rebecca's views on food. Of course John and Nicky didn't expect her to give up all her ideas – and she still believed in the beneficial effect of carrots and onions – but she did seem to be a little more prepared to accept that there was nothing really wrong with spaghetti, even if you put some rather thick sauce on it. And that, as far as John and Nicky were concerned, was a major breakthrough.

On the day before the wedding, Aunt Rebecca went so far as to cook them some of the ordinary spaghetti which Mr Pipelli had given her. She tasted it herself, and had to admit that it was delicious, even if not quite as delicious as her own carrot-flavoured variety.

'I suppose I should eat this from now on,' she said, a little bit hesitantly. 'After all, as from tomorrow I shall be the new Mrs Pipelli, and I shall have responsibilities towards the spaghetti industry.'

John tried not to catch Nicky's eye. If he did, he knew that it would be difficult not to smile.

The wedding was a splendid affair. Aunt Rebecca carried a bouquet of yellow flowers which Nicky had specially picked for her from the garden of Mr Pipelli's mansion, and Mr Pipelli beamed more than you would have thought it possible for anybody to beam. Outside, there were crowds of spaghetti workers who cheered lustily as the happy couple emerged.

'Well done!' they shouted in unison. 'And may you be happy for the rest of your lives.'

'Thank you, all,' responded Mr Pipelli. 'And take one week's extra holiday, starting today.'

This led to an even greater commotion, which brought the traffic to a standstill and made people for miles around open their windows to see what great event was happening.

John and Nicky watched all this, their hearts full of happiness. Then, as a large car drew up to take Mr Pipelli and Aunt Rebecca off on their honeymoon to Italy, John and Nicky joined the happy spaghetti workers to throw confetti on the newly-weds.

But it was not confetti they threw – it was spaghetti – which is an unusual thing to throw at a wedding. But on this occasion it was just right.

A selected list of titles available from Mammoth

While every effort is made to keep prices low, it is sometimes necessary to increase prices at short notice. Mandarin Paperbacks reserves the right to show new retail prices on covers which may differ from those previously advertised in the text or elsewhere.

The prices shown below were correct at the time of going to press.

☐	7497 0366 0	**Dilly the Dinosaur**	Tony Bradman	£2.50
☐	7497 0137 4	**Flat Stanley**	Jeff Brown	£2.50
☐	7497 0306 7	**The Chocolate Touch**	P Skene Catling	£2.50
☐	7497 0568 X	**Dorrie and the Goblin**	Patricia Coombs	£2.50
☐	7497 0114 5	**Dear Grumble**	W J Corbett	£2.50
☐	7497 0054 8	**My Naughty Little Sister**	Dorothy Edwards	£2.50
☐	7497 0723 2	**The Little Prince (colour ed.)**	A Saint-Exupery	£3.99
☐	7497 0305 9	**Bill's New Frock**	Anne Fine	£2.99
☐	7497 0590 6	**Wild Robert**	Diana Wynne Jones	£2.50
☐	7497 0661 9	**The Six Bullerby Children**	Astrid Lindgren	£2.50
☐	7497 0319 9	**Dr Monsoon Taggert's Amazing Finishing Academy**	Andrew Matthews	£2.50
☐	7497 0420 9	**I Don't Want To!**	Bel Mooney	£2.50
☐	7497 0833 6	**Melanie and the Night Animal**	Gillian Rubinstein	£2.50
☐	7497 0264 8	**Akimbo and the Elephants**	A McCall Smith	£2.50
☐	7497 0048 3	**Friends and Brothers**	Dick King-Smith	£2.50
☐	7497 0795 X	**Owl Who Was Afraid of the Dark**	Jill Tomlinson	£2.99

All these books are available at your bookshop or newsagent, or can be ordered direct from the publisher. Just tick the titles you want and fill in the form below.

Mandarin Paperbacks, Cash Sales Department, PO Box 11, Falmouth, Cornwall TR10 9EN.

Please send cheque or postal order, no currency, for purchase price quoted and allow the following for postage and packing:

UK including BFPO   £1.00 for the first book, 50p for the second and 30p for each additional book ordered to a maximum charge of £3.00.

Overseas including Eire   £2 for the first book, £1.00 for the second and 50p for each additional book thereafter.

NAME (Block letters) ....

ADDRESS ....

....

☐ I enclose my remittance for ....

☐ I wish to pay by Access/Visa Card Number

Expiry Date